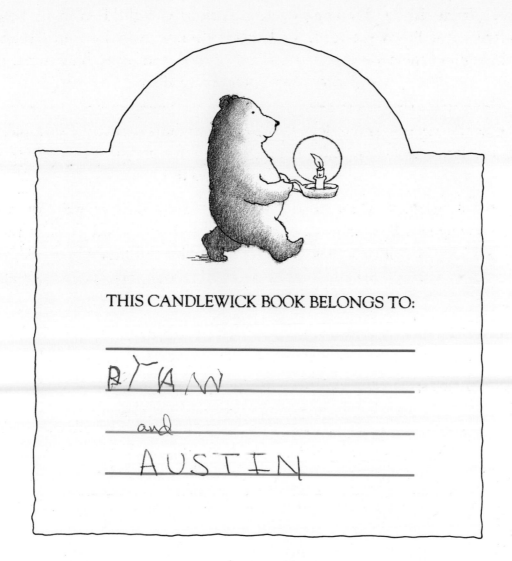

THIS CANDLEWICK BOOK BELONGS TO:

RYAN

and

AUSTIN

For Anna
M.W.

For Sebastian, David & C.P.
H.O.

Text copyright © 1991 by Martin Waddell
Illustrations copyright © 1991 by Helen Oxenbury

First U.S. paperback edition 1996

The Library of Congress has cataloged the hardcover edition as follows:

Waddell, Martin
Farmer duck/Martin Waddell, Helen Oxenbury.
Summary: When a kind and hardworking duck nearly collapses from
overwork, while taking care of a farm because the owner is too lazy to
do so, the rest of the animals get together and chase the farmer out of
town.
ISBN 1-56402-009-6 (hardcover)
[1. Domestic animals–Fiction.   2. Farm life–Fiction.]
I. Oxenbury, Helen, ill.   II. Title.
PZ7.W1137Far   1992
[E]–dc20   91-71855
ISBN 1-56402-596-9 (paperback)

10 9 8 7 6 5 4 3 2 1

Printed in Hong Kong

This book was typeset in Veronan Light Educational.
The pictures were done in watercolor

Candlewick Press
2067 Massachusetts Avenue
Cambridge, Massachusetts 02140

FARMER DUCK

written by

MARTIN WADDELL

illustrated by

HELEN OXENBURY

CANDLEWICK PRESS
CAMBRIDGE, MASSACHUSETTS

There once was a duck
who had the bad luck to live
with a lazy old farmer.
The duck did the work.
The farmer stayed
all day in bed.

The duck fetched the cow from the field.

"How goes the work?" called the farmer.

The duck answered,

"Quack!"

The duck brought the sheep from the hill.

"How goes the work?" called the farmer.

The duck answered,

"Quack!"

The duck put the hens in their house.

"How goes the work?"

called the farmer.

The duck answered,

"Quack!"

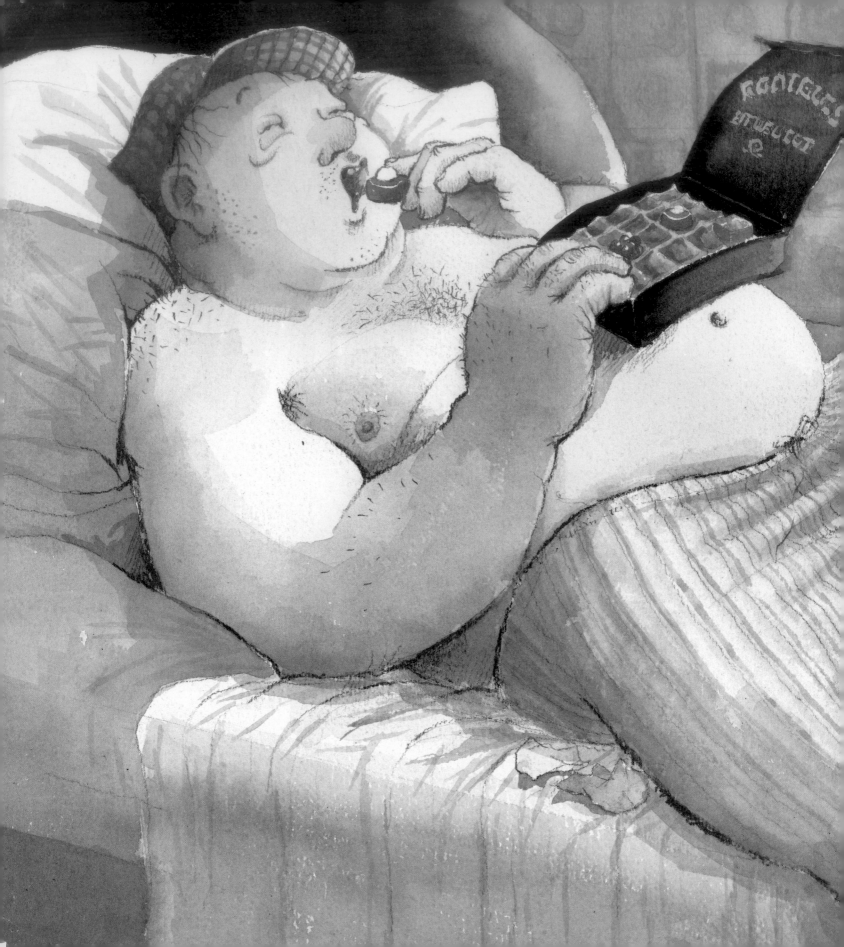

The farmer got fat through staying in bed,

and the poor duck got fed up

with working all day.

"How goes the work?"

"Quack!"

"How goes the work?"

"Quack!"

"How goes the work?"

"Quack!"

"How goes the work?"

"Quack!"

"How goes the work?"

"Quack!"

"How goes the work?"

"Quack!"

Soon, the poor duck grew
sleepy and weepy
and tired.

The hens and the cow and the
sheep got very upset.
They loved the duck.
So they held a meeting under
the moon, and they made
a plan for the morning.

"Moo!"

said the cow.

"Baa!"

said the sheep.

"Cluck!"

said the hens.

And *that* was the plan!

It was just before dawn and the farmyard was still.
Through the back door and into the house
crept the cow and the sheep
and the hens.

They stole
down the hall.
They creaked
up the stairs.

They squeezed under the bed of
the farmer and wriggled about.
The bed started to rock
and the farmer woke up,
and he called
"How goes the work?"
and...

"Moo!"

"Baa!"

"Cluck!"

They lifted his bed
and he started to shout,
and they banged and they bounced
the old farmer about and about and about,
right out of the bed...

and he fled with the cow and the sheep and the hens

mooing and baaing and clucking behind him.

Down the lane…

"Moo!"

through the fields…

"Baa!"

over the hill...

"Cluck!"

and he never came back.

The duck awoke and
waddled wearily into the
yard expecting to hear,
"How goes the work?"
But nobody spoke!

Then the cow and the sheep
and the hens came back.

"Quack?" asked the duck.

"Moo!" said the cow.

"Baa!" said the sheep.

"Cluck!" said the hens.

Which told the duck
the whole
story.

Then mooing and baaing
and clucking and quacking,
they all set to work
on their farm.

MARTIN WADDELL says that *Farmer Duck* is about justice, a concept that he believes is as important to children as it is to adults. "Children say 'It isn't fair!' and they mean it." One of the most prolific and successful children's writers of his time, Martin Waddell is the author of more than one hundred books for children, including *Can't You Sleep, Little Bear?, Let's Go Home, Little Bear, Owl Babies, The Big Big Sea, When the Teddy Bears Came, Once There Were Giants,* and *John Joe and the Big Hen.*

HELEN OXENBURY was drawn to *Farmer Duck* at once. "The plot appealed to me and gave me an extra edge to use in the illustrations." After a career in theater design, Helen Oxenbury turned to children's book illustration while expecting her first child, and has since won numerous awards for her splendid work. Her most recent books include *It's My Birthday, Tom and Pippo and the Bicycle,* and Trish Cooke's *So Much.*